W9-BNQ-420

A Stopwatch from Grampa

To Natalie, Cameron and Jim, and all the other great inspirations in my life.
And to Katie Scott and Anne Laurel Carter for their gentle guidance. — L.G.

In memory of my grampa and my papa — C.M.

Text © 2020 Loretta Garbutt
Illustrations © 2020 Carmen Mok

All rights reserved. No part of this publication may be reproduced, stored
in a retrieval system or transmitted, in any form or by any means, without the prior written
permission of Kids Can Press Ltd. or, in case of photocopying or other reprographic copying,
a license from The Canadian Copyright Licensing Agency (Access Copyright). For an Access
Copyright license, visit www.accesscopyright.ca or call toll free to 1-800-893-5777.

Kids Can Press gratefully acknowledges the financial support of the Government of Ontario,
through Ontario Creates; the Ontario Arts Council; the Canada Council for the Arts; and the
Government of Canada for our publishing activity.

Published in Canada and the U.S. by Kids Can Press Ltd.
25 Dockside Drive, Toronto, ON M5A 0B5

Kids Can Press is a Corus Entertainment Inc. company

www.kidscanpress.com

The artwork in this book was rendered in gouache and color
and graphite pencils, and was edited digitally in Photoshop.
The text is set in Amasis.

Edited by Katie Scott
Designed by Marie Bartholomew

Printed and bound in Malaysia in 10/2019 by Tien Wah Press (Pte) Ltd.

CM 20 0 9 8 7 6 5 4 3 2 1

Library and Archives Canada Cataloguing in Publication

Title: A stopwatch from Grampa / written by Loretta Garbutt ; illustrated by Carmen Mok.
Names: Garbutt, Loretta, 1961– author. | Mok, Carmen, 1968– illustrator.
Identifiers: Canadiana 20190106972 | ISBN 9781525301445 (hardcover)
Classification: LCC PS8613.A688 S76 2020 | DDC jC813/.6 — dc23

A Stopwatch from Grampa

Loretta Garbutt   Carmen Mok

Kids Can Press

When summer started, I got Grampa's stopwatch.

I don't want his stopwatch. I want him.

Grampa used to time everything.

He timed me when I raced to the end of our street and back. Best speed: 24 seconds.

He timed me eating bubblegum ice cream: 1 minute, 58 seconds. Brain freeze: 6 seconds.

Sitting on a log in the park, we timed a swallowtail caterpillar crawling up my pant leg: 7 minutes, 22 seconds.

The stopwatch was Grampa's favorite thing.

I can't believe he left it behind.

Sometimes, I timed Grampa: 5 minutes to eat three oatmeal raisin cookies. And 18 long minutes to drink his coffee, sip by sip.

Curled up on the couch after dinner, he snored
for a whole 20 minutes, then laughed for 12 seconds
when I told him he sounded like a velociraptor.

It isn't fair that the watch is still here when he's not.
I click it on, off, on, off. Then I throw the dumb thing
into my drawer.

Now there are no more Grampa minutes,
Grampa seconds.
Time just stops.

When school starts, everything feels different.

Playing soccer at recess isn't fun anymore.

Lunch with my friends is boring. I don't even want to go to the park after school.

Maybe I shouldn't have told Grampa he snored like a dinosaur.

I remember the first time Grampa let me hold his stopwatch.
He clicked the silver button on top, and we watched the red
hand move round and round. I couldn't take my eyes off it.

"Seconds tick by quickly," Grampa said.

He clicked the silver button again, and the watch stopped.

Another button reset the hand back to zero.

"But you can always start over again."

I didn't think about the stopwatch for a long time.

Then one day, I find it buried under my red sweater.

It fits perfectly in my hand.

I crawl into bed and click the silver button. *Tick, tick, tick …*

It takes 48 minutes for the shadows to move across the room.

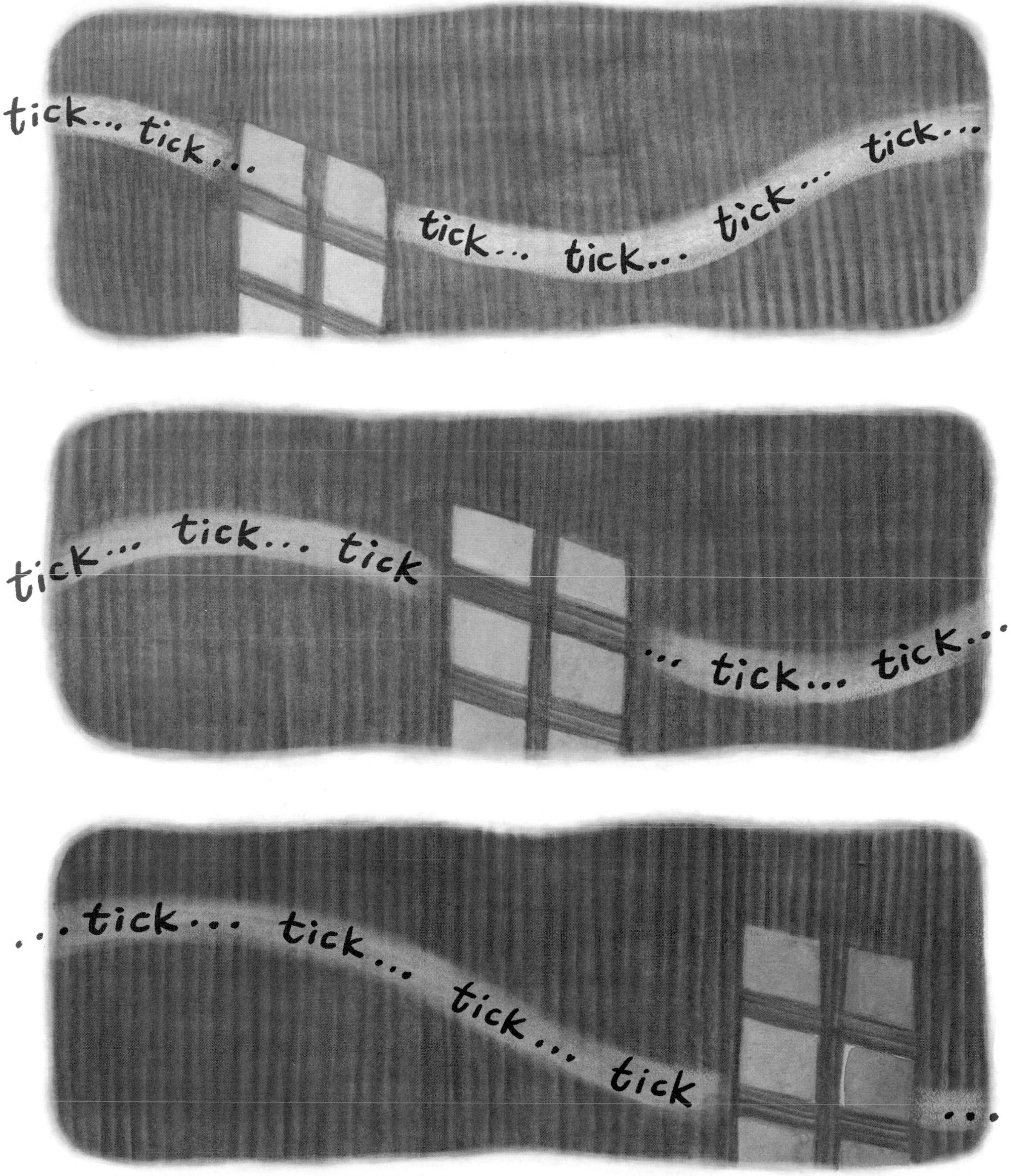
tick... tick...
tick... tick... tick... tick...
tick... tick... tick
... tick... tick...
...tick... tick... tick... tick
...

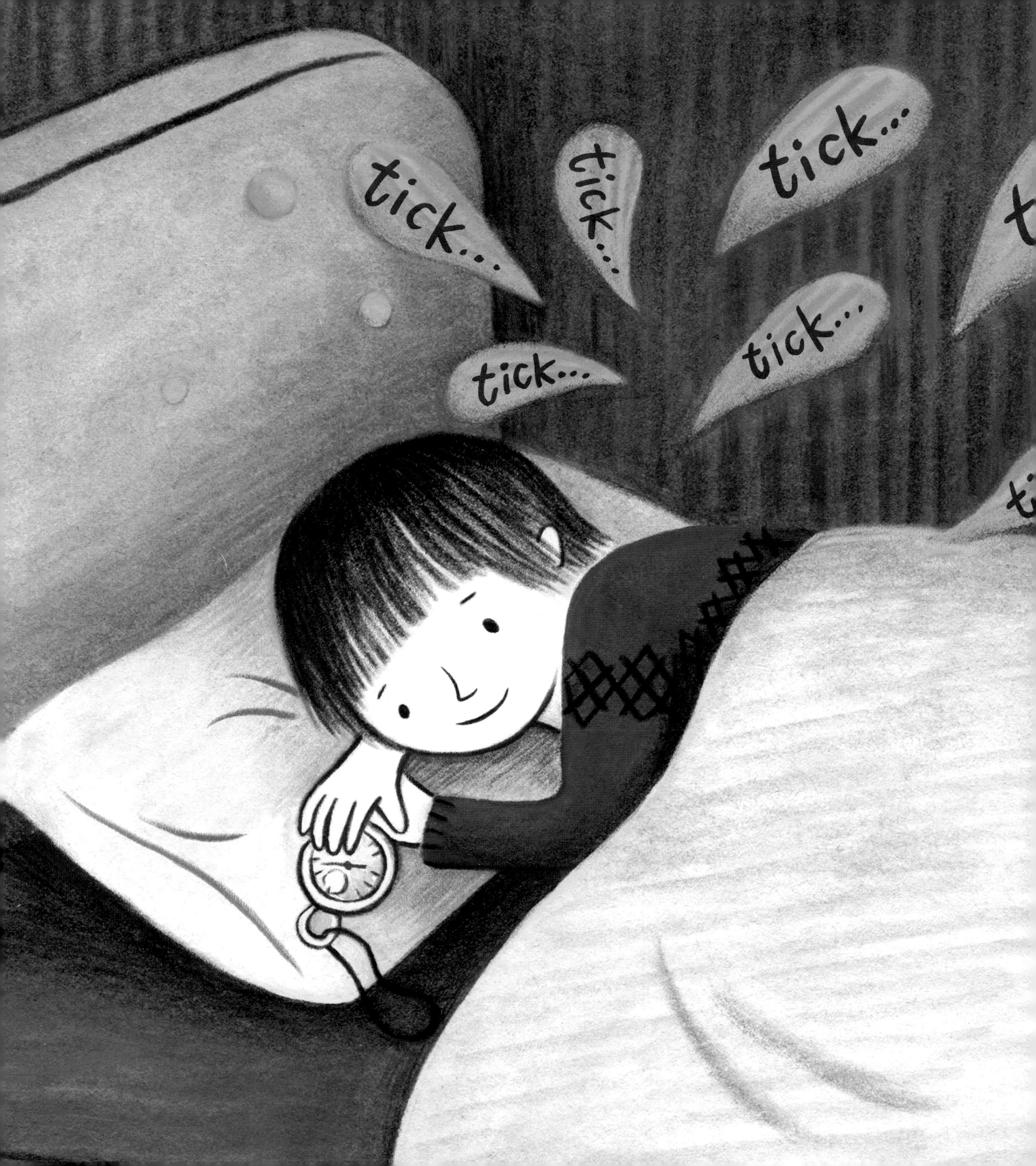
tick...
tick...
tick...
tick...
tick...

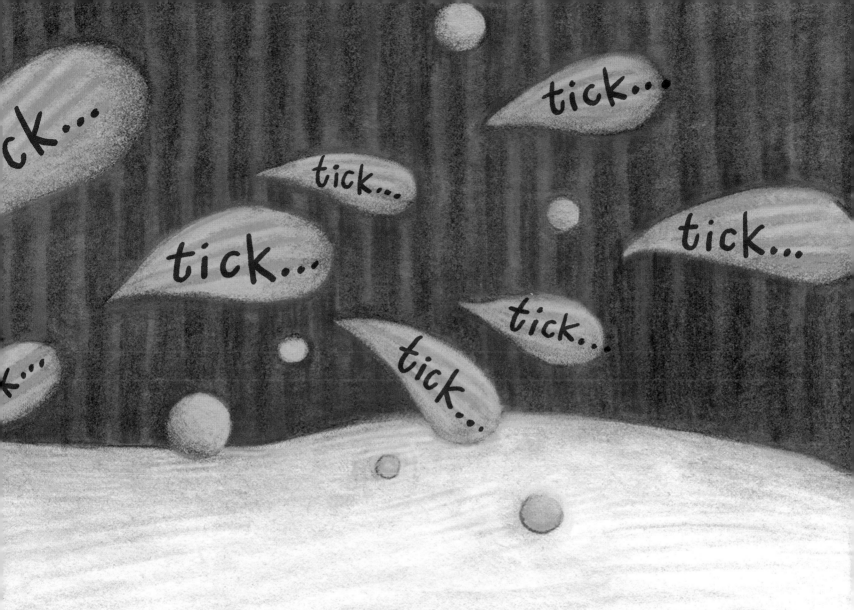

The watch sounds like Grampa. It makes me think of
all the things we used to time together. Remembering
him feels good.

Tick, tick, tick …

Like he is still here with me.

When the smell of oatmeal raisin cookies fills
my room, I hop out of bed and run downstairs:
a quick 6 seconds to get to the kitchen.

I wonder if I can eat three cookies in 4 minutes.
I'll need some help to find out.